COLIN DANN

The Further Adventures of
The Animals of Farthing Wood

BBC CHILDREN'S BOOKS

The Great Stag welcomed the animals of Farthing Wood to White Deer Park after their long journey.

Winter arrived abruptly and food was hard to find. Most of the inhabitants of the Reserve were friendly, but Scarface and his mate, Lady Blue, resented the intrusion of the newcomers and prevented them from hunting on their territory.

The Farthing Wood animals remembered their Oath and helped one another survive.

Late one afternoon as Badger was foraging for food, he lost his way in the snow and had a bad fall.

The other animals looked for him in vain.

Fortunately Badger was rescued by the Park Warden and taken to his cottage to recover. There Badger befriended the Warden's cat and told him his story. He persuaded the cat to take a message to his friends, since he knew they would be worried about him.

Cat soon found Mole, who was delighted at the news that Badger was safe.

Kestrel, flying overhead, saw the cat and thought Mole was in danger. She swooped to Mole's rescue and attacked the cat before Mole could prevent her.

"You've made a mistake," Mole cried. "The cat has brought news of Badger!"

But the injured cat was not appeased and vowed revenge.

Badger eventually recovered from his injury. The cat kept him company on his journey home.

Kestrel had been watching for Badger and flew down to welcome him. The cat saw his chance for revenge and pounced.

Badger at once defended Kestrel, but remembering the cat's helpfulness to him, allowed him to escape.

The other animals, overjoyed at Badger's return, ran to greet him.

Towards the end of winter the Warden was taken to hospital. Then the animals faced a new danger as poachers came each night to the Park to hunt the deer.

Fox thought of a clever plan to foil the poachers. He saved the deer and rid the Park of the threat.

By the time Spring arrived, the Warden was back in his cottage fit and well again. Cubs were born to both Vixen and Lady Blue. Scarface taunted his mate by saying he thought Vixen's cubs were stronger than hers.

Scarface became so envious that he watched Fox's family's every move. One day while the exhausted Vixen was sleeping, Scarface leaped on the weakest of her cubs, Dreamer, and killed her.

Fox was too distraught to act, but the biggest of his cubs, Bold, was determined to avenge his sister's death. He ran rashly into Scarface's territory, but was quickly cornered by the blue foxes.

Bold managed to escape. Meanwhile his father and brother were ambushed by the blue foxes while on their way to rescue him.

The White Stag intervened to prevent further bloodshed.
  Fox was enraged by Bold's foolishness, and insisted on his
obedience in future, but Bold, determined to be independent,
decided to leave the Park.

Beyond the Park's boundaries, Bold discovered a whole new world. A crow watched him from a branch.

"What are you doing out in the daylight? Don't you know humans are around?"

Bold ignored him and carried on until he reached a copse, where he found shelter in a badger's set for the night. At dawn the set's owner, Shadow, returned, and the two made friends.

Within the Park the feud between Scarface and the Farthing Wood animals worsened. Scarface had begun to pick off the weaker creatures. The Farthing Wood animals decided that they must be on their guard and keep watch.

While Fox's cub, Charmer, was keeping a look-out one day, she encountered one of the blue fox cubs called Ranger. The two young foxes were attracted to each other despite their parents' rivalry.

Life outside the Park had its share of danger. One day Bold found Shadow caught in a trap. In the process of freeing her, the spring flew back, wounding him badly in the eye.

The dangers in the wood prompted Bold to leave, but soon he found himself in greater peril. Blundering into a pheasant shoot, he became a target, and was badly lamed.

Back in White Deer Park the Farthing Wood animals
had decided in desperation to call on Adder to rid them
of Scarface. Unfortunately they chose Weasel as their
messenger. She muddled the message, and Adder killed
Scarface's son, Bounder, by mistake.

Scarface was determined to hunt down his son's killer, but
Adder went into hiding.

When the Farthing Wood animals discovered Adder's error, they feared retribution and doubled their guard on the boundaries.

Meanwhile Ranger and Charmer continued to meet without their families' knowledge.

Bold meanwhile lay injured, unable to hunt for himself.
The Crow whom he had met during his first day of freedom
outside of the Park reappeared, and now Bold asked him for
help. The Crow flew to fetch Shadow, who brought food.

Bold hated being dependent on his friends, so Crow suggested he could survive better in the nearby town, where there were rich pickings to be had from human left-overs.

Back in White Deer Park Charmer was in trouble with her family for her friendship with Ranger. Vixen persuaded Fox to talk with the blue cub.

"Our families are sworn enemies," Fox said to Ranger. "Where would you stand in the event of a battle?"

"I promise that I would not fight against you," Ranger replied.

The Farthing Wood animals were to suffer another blow.
Badger's extreme age caught up with him and he died
peacefully, surrounded by his friends.

Bold meantime had found a new friend in the town – a vixen called Whisper. She noticed Bold's injuries and realized he needed help.

Whisper took Bold to a favourite hunting place where together they caught many rats.

Bold was invited to share her den in a churchyard.

Crow remained friends. Hunting was still a problem for
Bold, but they encountered Rollo, a lonely St Bernard,
who in exchange for their company, offered to share his food
with them.

Some time later Whisper broke the good news to Bold that she was expecting their cubs. She told him she wanted them to be born in White Deer Park, where they could live in safety.

Bold was reluctant to return, but despite his lame leg agreed
to lead her there. In her eagerness, Whisper tended to force
the pace.

Bold's injuries had left him very weak and he eventually collapsed with the effort. While Whisper was away hunting, he was attacked by a pack of dogs.

Happily Crow had tracked Bold's progress, and had returned to the town to enlist Rollo's help. He was just returning with Rollo when they saw the attack, and between them they put the dogs to flight.

The foxes' feud within the Park came to a head when Lady Blue attacked Vixen.

Fox was outraged by Vixen's wounds . . .

as was Scarface by his own mate's suffering. The angry blue fox vowed to wipe out the Farthing Wood animals once and for all.

Remembering his promise, Ranger quickly brought warning of the attack, and the animals took refuge together in Fox's earth.

Scarface and his pack arrived in force and threatened to starve the animals into submission.

Fox at once invited Scarface to single combat.

Fox's youth was on his side and he soon had Scarface at his mercy.

Suddenly Kestrel spied the Warden approaching and Fox released Scarface, who sloped away.

Bold and Whisper had at last arrived within sight of the Park's
boundaries. Bold was too weak to carry on. He sent Whisper
for food and in her absence hid himself.

"One last favour," Bold said to Crow. "Don't tell Whisper where I am. I can't go back to the Park."

Crow kept his word. When Whisper returned with food, he pretended he didn't know where Bold was. Heartbroken, Whisper went on alone and entered the Park.

One of the Farthing Wood animals had not been content to leave Scarface alive. Adder had lain in wait for Scarface in the stream and as the blue fox swam across, she had sunk her fangs into him.

Only Lady Blue and her cubs mourned Scarface's passing.

Charmer found Whisper just within the boundary and took her to Fox and Vixen. Whisper explained why she had come and was welcomed.

　She told them of Bold's plight and they hastily set off in search of him, while Whisper stayed with Charmer.

Crow led them to Bold's hideout.
  "Whisper has told us everything," Vixen said lovingly.
"Dear Bold, your cubs will be safe with us."
  Bold was thankful. "My task is done," he said.

"You're a brave and honourable creature," Fox told him.
"I'm proud you're my son."
Bold could at last die in peace.

With the union of Ranger and Charmer, the emnity between the two families of foxes came to an end and harmony was restored, once more, to White Deer Park.

Published by BBC Children's Books
a division of BBC Enterprises Limited, 80 Wood Lane, London W12 0TT
First published 1993

The original books in the *Animals of Farthing Wood* series are published by
Reed Children's Books and Random House Children's Books

ISBN 0 563 40323 3

Set in Palatino by BBC Children's Books
Printed and bound in Belgium by Proost NV
Colour separation by Dot Gradations Ltd, Chelmsford
Cover printed in Belgium by Proost NV
Reprinted 1994